A Kiss for Lily

Written by Lia Nirgad

Illustrated by Yossi Abulafia

MacAdam/Cage Children's Books
155 Sansome Street, Suite 550
San Francisco, CA 94104
www.macadamcage.com

Library of Congress Cataloging-in-Publication Data

Nirgad, Lia.
A kiss for Lily / by Lia Nirgad ; illustrated by Yossi Abulafia.
p. cm.
Summary: Lily the giraffe wants a kiss on the cheek just like the one
Michael received from his father, but she is so very, very tall finding
someone to kiss her will not be easy.

ISBN 1-59692-163-3 (hardcover : alk. paper)
[1. Giraffe–Fiction. 2. Kissing–Fiction. 3. Animals–Fiction.]
I. Abulafia, Yossi, ill. II. Title.
PZ7.N628Kis 2005
[E]–dc22
                                        2005013466

Printed in China.

1 2 3 4 5 6 7 8 9 10

A Kiss for Lily

Written by Lia Nirgad

Illustrated by Yossi Abulafia

MacAdam/Cage Children's Books

Lily the giraffe lives in a park next to Michael's house.
Lily has long, long legs, and a long, long, long neck
covered with brown spots.

Lily's neck is so long, her head reaches all the way
up to the top of the tallest trees in the park.

Lily's neck is so long, she can eat
the highest, greenest leaves—
the ones she likes best.

Usually Lily is very happy to be so tall.
She likes looking down and seeing everyone, and
she likes talking to the birds who live in the trees.

One day Lily saw Michael getting
a kiss on the cheek from his daddy.
She wanted a kiss too.

Oscar the dog was just passing by. Lily asked him, "Please give me a kiss on the cheek." Oscar answered, "You're much too tall for me to reach your cheek." He ran off to look for bones.

A little while later Maggie the cat came by. Lily asked her, "Please give me a kiss on the cheek." Maggie answered, "You're much too tall for me to reach your cheek." She ran off to look for mice.

Then Lily called out to the orange bird who lives on a tree's highest branch, and asked her for a kiss on the cheek. The orange bird kissed her. Lily didn't like that kiss one bit. The orange bird had a sharp, hard beak, and Lily wanted a soft kiss just like the one Michael got from his daddy.

Then Michael came by. Lily asked him, "Please give me a kiss on the cheek." Michael said, "My sweet Lily, I'll be very happy to give you a kiss."

Michael stretched up and stood on
his tiptoes, but Lily was so tall.
She was soooooo tall.
She was so very, very, very tall.
Michael couldn't reach her cheek.

Michael said to Lily, "You're too tall for me.
Could you please bend your neck down just a bit?"
Lily, who really wanted her kiss, bent down as far
as she could. But she was so tall.
She was soooooo tall.
She was so very, very, very tall that even though
she tried and tried, her head was still too high for
Michael's kiss.

Michael ran home and brought a chair.
He put the chair next to Lily
and climbed up and stretched,
and stood on his tiptoes.

But Lily was so tall.

She was soooooo tall.

She was so very, very, very tall,

that he couldn't reach her cheek.

Michael ran home and brought a table.
He put the table right next to Lily
and climbed on the table
and climbed on the chair
and stretched up and stood on his tiptoes.

But Lily was so tall.
She was soooooo tall.
She was so very, very, very tall
that he couldn't reach her cheek.

Michael ran home and brought his bed.
He put the bed right next to Lily.
He climbed on the bed,
and climbed on the table,
and climbed on the chair,
and stretched up and stood on his tiptoes.

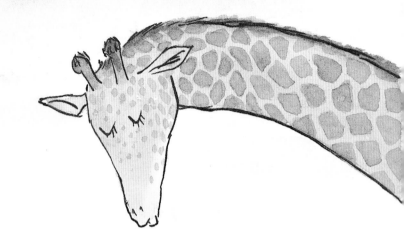

But Lily was so tall.
She was soooooo tall.
She was so very, very, very tall
that he couldn't reach her cheek.

Michael was sad.

He so wanted to give Lily a kiss.

He sat down under a tree and thought.

He thought and thought.

And he sat and sat.

And Michael thought some more.

Finally he knew just what to do.

Quickly he began to climb the tree.
He climbed some more,
and then higher and higher,
until he came to a place he'd never
been before.

High above the lower branches,
high above the middle branches,
high above the highest branches,
higher even than the very, very highest branches,
he finally reached Lily's cute face.

Michael gave Lily a kiss on the cheek. It was so nice,
he gave her a kiss on the other cheek too.
And that was so very, very nice, he gave her a kiss
on each eye as well.

Lily smiled and licked Michael's face
and then happily shut her eyes and went to sleep
dreaming of Michael's sweet, warm kisses.

Michael realized how late it was. He quickly climbed down the tree and hurried home to dinner, where, just as always, he got a kiss on each eye from his daddy.